KT-104-664

Copyright © 2019

make believe ideas ltd

The Wilderness, Berkhamsted, Hertfordshire, HP4 2AZ, UK.

All rights reserved. No part of this publication may be reproduced, stored in a retrieval system, or transmitted in any form or by any means, electronic, mechanical, photocopying, recording, or otherwise, without the prior written permission of the copyright owner.

www.makebelieveideas.com

Written by Rosie Greening.
Illustrated by Lara Ede.

# Meghan Sparkle and the ROYAL Baby

Lara Ede • Rosie Greening

make
believe
ideas

Once, in **Coral Kingdom**, an announcement came to say that a brand-new **royal baby** had been born that very day!

Almost all the mermaids thought the baby news was great.
But Princess Meghan Sparkle didn't want to celebrate.
Hooray!
Yay!

She was baby Bubble's **sister**, but she found it all a **bore**.
From *Meghan's* point of view, her life was going **fine** before!

…and always found a **quiet** place
to **read** or have a **doze**.

But now, the baby **screamed** so much,
it drove her up the wall,
and **smelled** so bad that *Meghan*
couldn't concentrate at all!

Wahhhhhhhhhh!
Calming sea sounds

One day, Meghan couldn't wait
to read her book somewhere,
when suddenly the sound of
Bubble's **crying** filled the air.

So Meghan searched for
somewhere **far away** from
all the noise,

but every room
was **smelly**...

full...
or stuffed with baby toys!

She slammed her book closed with a **SMACK** and shouted,

**"IT'S NOT FAIR!**

Everyone's gone baby mad: I can't read ANYWHERE."

She sped outside and swam along
a winding path at speed,
until she found a silent spot:
the **PERFECT** place to read!

Meghan read her book for **hours**,
as **happy** as a clam.

But **when** she tried to leave,
she cried…

She'd swum out here too **quickly**,
and forgotten to keep track.
So now she simply **didn't know**
which path would take her back!

Just when she felt **all at sea**,
the princess heard a cough.
The **mail-turtle** was swimming by,
dropping parcels off.

**"Your Royal Highness!"** Turtle cried,
and gave a little bow.

"Can you help me?" **Meghan** asked.
"I've **lost my way** somehow!"

"**I'll take you home,**" said Turtle, "but I **must** drop off this mail."
"**That sounds fun!**" the mermaid said, and joined him on his trail.

First, he had a parcel for the **clownfish** family,
who all lived **cramped together** in a small anemone.

"That looks **crowded**," *Meghan* thought,
and watched the clownfish play.
"I'm **lucky** I don't share a room
with Bubble every day."

A choir **singing** whale songs
was the next stop on their rounds.

But *Meghan* couldn't **understand**
the group's **unusual** sounds.

Turtle laughed:
"That's how they **speak**:
it just sounds odd to **you**."

*Meghan* thought of **Bubble's cries**...
could they mean something too?

They went to **Seaweed Stables** for their last delivery.
The little baby seahorses were racing with a
"Wheeeeee!"
This is fun!
I was born to win!

Meghan and the turtle
watched the babies for a while.

"Maybe siblings **are** ok,"
thought Meghan with a smile.

With the packages delivered,
**Meghan** thought of what she'd seen.
And **suddenly** she realised
how **silly** she had been!

She said, "I **understand** now
that when all is said and done,
having someone **new** around
is going to be **fun!**"

The turtle guided **Meghan** back across the ocean floor,
and soon she heard a distant cry she **knew** she'd heard before.

"Thank you, Turtle!"
Meghan said.
"I recognise those sounds."
And then she followed Bubble's cries
into the castle grounds.

She rushed to **hug** the baby, feeling happy as can be.
"Hello Bubble," *Meghan* said. "I'm glad we're family."

After that, she didn't leave the royal baby's side,
and read her **favourite** books aloud
whenever Bubble cried.

So Meghan found some lovely friends, and as young Bubble grew,

she saw that life is wonderful when you are one of two!